GPJC
3/19

# CALLIE ASKS FOR HELP

Based on the episode written by Mike Kramer
Adapted by Annie Auerbach
Illustrated by Marco Bucci

**ABDOPUBLISHING.COM**

Reinforced library bound edition published in 2019 by Spotlight, a division of ABDO, PO Box 398166, Minneapolis, Minnesota 55439. Spotlight produces high-quality reinforced library bound editions for schools and libraries. Published by agreement with Disney Press, an imprint of Disney Book Group.

Printed in the United States of America, North Mankato, Minnesota.
042018      092018

**DISNEY PRESS**
New York • Los Angeles

THIS BOOK CONTAINS
RECYCLED MATERIALS

Library of Congress Control Number: 2017961157

Publisher's Cataloging in Publication Data

Names: Auerbach, Annie, author. | Kramer, Mike, author. | Bucci, Marco, illustrator.
Title: Sheriff Callie's Wild West: Callie asks for help / by Annie Auerbach and Mike Kramer; illustrated by Marco Bucci.
Description: Minneapolis, MN : Spotlight, 2019 | Series: World of reading level pre-1
Summary: Callie and Spark end up stuck at the bottom of a deep canyon after trying to help too many townsfolk at once. Who will come to Sheriff Callie's rescue?
Identifiers: ISBN 9781532141843 (lib. bdg.)
Subjects: LCSH: Sheriff Callie's Wild West (Television program)--Juvenile fiction. | Western stories--Juvenile fiction. | Sheriffs--Juvenile fiction. | Helping behavior--Juvenile fiction. | Readers (Primary)--Juvenile fiction.
Classification: DDC [E]--dc23

**Spotlight**
A Division of ABDO
abdopublishing.com

Sheriff Callie likes to help.
Sparky likes to help, too.

"Help!" yells Farmer Stinky.
It's Callie and Sparky to the rescue.

Callie helps Farmer Stinky.
They paint the barn.

More friends need help.

# Go, Callie! Go, Sparky!

Callie and Sparky help Dirty Dan.
They move a big rock.

Callie helps Priscilla.
She finds Priscilla's hat.

Ella asks for help.

There is a fight at her saloon.

Bo asks for help.

His jackalopes ran away!

Go, Callie! Go, Sparky!

Which milk shake is best?
Strawberry or banana?
No one can agree.
Callie mixes them together. Yum!

The jackalopes are getting away!

Callie brings them back.

Callie and Sparky run back and forth.

Sparky's feet dig a hole.

The hole becomes a canyon.

Soon Callie and Sparky are stuck!

Callie throws her lasso.
It does not work.

They jump up high.
But it is not high enough.

They are still stuck.
Callie and Sparky need help!

Callie writes a note on her hat.
She asks for help.

Please HELP! We are stuck in a deep canyon! Sheriff Callie and Sparky

They send the hat into the air.

Go, hat!

The hat lands on Peck!

Peck calls his friends.

"Callie and Sparky need help!" he says.

They find Callie and Sparky.
How can they help?

Callie throws the lasso.
Everyone helps pull.

Callie and Sparky are safe!
"Thank you," says Callie.
She is happy she asked for help.

This place has a new name.
It is called Helping Hand Canyon!